Mopoke.

PHILIP BUNTING

SCHOLASTIC

This is a mopoke.

This is a highpoke.

This is a lowpoke.

This is a poshpoke.

This is a poorpoke.

This is two pokes.

This is more pokes.

This is a weepoke.

Fee-fi-fo-poke.

This is a yo-poke.

This is a yo!-poke.

This is a wombat.

This is a mo'poke.

This is a ’fropoke.

This is a snowpoke.

This is a glowpoke.

This is a slowpoke.

This is a crowpoke.

This is a blowpoke.

Woahpoke!

ENOUGH!

Nopoke.

FOR FLORENCE,
WITH LOVE XX

'Mopoke' is the Australian nickname for the Southern Boobook, their smallest and most common species of owl. Mopokes are known for their love of peace and quiet, and for their eponymous 'mo-poke' call.

First published in 2017 by Omnibus Books
An imprint of Scholastic Australia Pty Limited

First published in the UK in 2017 by Scholastic Children's Books
Euston House, 24 Eversholt Street
London NW1 1DB
a division of Scholastic Ltd
www.scholastic.co.uk
London ~ New York ~ Toronto ~ Sydney ~ Auckland
Mexico City ~ New Delhi ~ Hong Kong

ISBN 978 1407 18074 8

Printed in China

1 3 5 7 9 10 8 6 4 2